PUFFIN BOOKS

Peril at the Pirate S

Tony Bradman was born and grew up in South
London. After leaving university, he became a
journalist and worked in the music press for
several years. He then became Deputy Editor of
Parents magazine, where he began to review
children's books. He soon began writing his own,
and published his first in 1984. In 1987 he gave up
journalism to write for children full-time. He has
written fiction and poetry, and edited a number of
anthologies. He reviews for the *Daily Telegraph*,
and lives in London with his wife and three
children.

Peril at the Pirate School

Tony Bradman

Illustrated by Rowan Barnes Murphy

PUFFIN BOOKS

PUFFIN BOOKS

Published by the Penguin Group
27 Wrights Lane, London W8 5TZ, England
Viking Penguin Inc., 40 West 23rd Street, New York, New York 10010, USA
Penguin Books Australia Ltd, Ringwood, Victoria, Australia
Penguin Books Canada Ltd, 2801 John Street, Markham, Ontario, Canada L3R 1B4
Penguin Books (NZ) Ltd, 182–190 Wairau Road, Auckland 10, New Zealand

Penguin Books Ltd, Registered Offices: Harmondsworth, Middlesex, England

First published by Piccadilly Press Ltd 1990
Published in Puffin Books 1991
5 7 9 10 8 6 4

Text copyright © Tony Bradman, 1990
Illustrations copyright © Rowan Barnes Murphy, 1990
All rights reserved

Made and printed in Great Britain by
Richard Clay Ltd, Bungay, Suffolk

Chapter One

In which goodbyes are said

It was a lovely day. The sun was shining,
and a good, strong breeze filled the sails of
our ship, The Saucy Sally.

But I wasn't very happy. In fact, I was
just about as miserable as a pirate boy can
be. We were heading for the island of
Santa Brenda, and once we arrived, my
days of fun on The Saucy Sally would be
over.

My big sister Molly and I were being sent
to a boarding school. And that was

1

something I definitely wasn't looking forward to.

'Hard to port, First Mate!' called out my father, Cap'n Bluebeard. He was scanning the horizon with his spyglass. 'Heading north by north east!'

'Aye aye, Cap'n,' replied my mother, the First Mate. She was at her usual place, behind The Saucy Sally's big wheel.

Father put his spyglass away and turned to Molly and me.

'Now, Jim and Molly,' he said, 'we'll be there soon, so all hands look lively! Do ye go below and make sure your kit's ready. Ye can both change into clean sea jerseys, too.'

'That's right,' said the First Mate, 'you want to look your best on the first day.'

'We don't,' said Molly. 'And we don't want to go to a stupid old boarding school either, do we, Jim?'

I opened my mouth, but I didn't get a
chance to say anything.

'Belay that talk!' shouted the Cap'n. He
sounded very cross. 'Shiver me timbers,
Molly, we've been through it all before,
and our minds are made up. Why, as soon
as I read about that there new school I
knew it were the place for the both of 'ee.'

'But *why* can't we stay on board with
you?' said Molly. 'We do lessons every
day.'

'Ah, Molly,' said the First Mate. 'You and your brother do your lessons when it suits you, and that's not very often. The rest of the time you spend bickering.'

It was true. Molly and I were always trying to get out of doing our lessons. There was usually something else much more exciting to do . . . And we *had* been fighting a lot lately.

'The First Mate's right,' said the Cap'n. 'Ye both need better teachin' than your old ma and pa can give ye. And perhaps a spell in a good school will teach 'ee some proper pirate behaviour.'

'But...' said Molly.

'I'll have no more of your "buts", Molly Bluebeard,' roared the Cap'n. 'Ye are going to Miss Prudence Proper's Academy for Pirate Pupils, and that's an end of it. *Now get ye below*!'

Molly stamped off down the

4

companionway to our cabin with her nose
in the air. I followed.

'Parents!' she hissed when the door was
shut. 'They know they'll miss us . . . I
heard them talking about it last night when
they came to tuck us into our hammocks.
They thought we were asleep, but I
wasn't.'

I hadn't been asleep either, so I'd heard
them talking, too. They'd sounded quite
upset about sending us to school. But that
wasn't going to stop them doing it. There
was no point in arguing.

So Molly and I got changed and checked
our kit bags as we'd been told. Then we
went back on deck.

A little while later we arrived at Santa Brenda. We dropped anchor in the harbour. Molly and I said goodbye to Trelawney the parrot, and Long John Rover, our dog. Then we all got into the dinghy, and the First Mate rowed us ashore. It didn't take us long to find the school, worse luck.

Miss Prudence Proper herself met us at the gate. I'd never seen anyone quite like her before. She was tall and bony, and she had a big, hooked nose. There were a couple of hairy warts right on the end of it. She smiled at us, and I wished she hadn't. Some of her teeth were missing, some were green, and the rest were black.

Standing next to her was a giant of a pirate with an enormous beard and funny, piggy, little eyes.

''Tis Jim and Molly isn't it? Welcome aboard!' said Miss Prudence.

Molly and I didn't say anything, even though the Cap'n nudged us from behind.

'Don't worry,' said Miss Prudence to our parents. 'I can see they're a little shy. But they'll soon settle in. Jasper, carry those kit bags for Master and Mistress Bluebeard. There's only one cabin empty, so I'm afraid you'll have to share . . .'

Jasper was obviously the huge pirate. He picked up our bags in one gigantic hand, and led the way into the school.

As we walked along, Miss Prudence explained that the school was run like a pirate ship. We soon saw what she meant. For a start, it actually *looked* like one. There was a galley instead of a kitchen, too, a mess-hall for school dinners, and the corridors were called companionways. The room we'd be sleeping in was called a cabin, and it had hammocks, not beds. There were portholes instead of windows.

At last it was time to say goodbye. The Cap'n and the First Mate gave Molly and me a hug and kiss each, and told us to be good. I felt a hot tear trickle down my cheek.

'Now, now, Jim lad,' said the Cap'n with a sniff. He pulled out a big handkerchief and blew his nose. 'Belay that there blubbin' . . . ye'll have me howling too.'

All too soon they were gone, leaving us in the care of Miss Prudence and Jasper.

For some reason, that made me feel very uneasy . . .

Chapter Two

In which Jim gets a note

The next day Molly and I were both up very early. To tell the truth, neither of us had slept well. We were both feeling homesick. For once I think we were glad to be together.

At least we didn't have much time to worry about the way we felt. As soon as we were washed and dressed, Jasper came to take us to breakfast in the mess-hall.

The food was very good. There were

plenty of pirate cereals, big barrels of ship's biscuits, and lashings of mango juice. But I didn't eat or drink very much, even though I was pretty hungry. I was too busy looking at the other children.

I recognised a few from some of the pirate parties Molly and I had been to. I could see Polly and Pat, Captain Flint's daughters, and Tom and Tim, the Teach brothers, sitting next to them. I waved, but they didn't wave back. They just looked down at their bowls as if they didn't know me.

We'd always been friendly, so it was strange for them to act that way. But that wasn't the only strange thing going on. Molly had noticed it too.

'Psst!' she whispered in my ear. 'Why isn't anybody *talking*?'

The only sounds were the clunk of spoons on wooden bowls and the

occasional cough. And there was something else, too — everyone was well-behaved!

I remember the Cap'n once said that pirate children plus pirate children equals trouble. But the pupils of Miss Prudence Proper's Pirate Academy had obviously never heard of that sum. No one was laughing or arguing. No one was flicking food or sticking out their tongues. No one was even slurping or spilling anything down their fronts.

'It's not natural!' whispered Molly. She was right, and I was about to say so when a sudden noise stopped me.

'Who be blabbin' down there on the lower deck?' somebody roared. It was a teacher, and he was staring at us from a table at the other end of the mess-hall. All the teachers were sitting there.

'Steady, Mr Thunder,' said Miss Prudence. 'Those are our new pupils, and they don't know all the rules yet. Talking isn't allowed at meal times, Jim and Molly.'

'Sorry, Miss Prudence,' said Molly. She nudged me with her elbow, and I said sorry too. Mr Thunder took his eyes off us and started eating again, but I couldn't stop looking at him or the other teachers on the top table.

If they'd been a real pirate crew, I'd have said you couldn't have met a scurvier band of rogues. Mr Thunder, for instance, had

13

the meanest, most vicious face I'd ever come across. The others — most of whom had peg-legs, patches or hooks — all looked as if they'd skin you alive for fun.

But as they were teachers, I wasn't quite sure *what* to think.

After breakfast I had my chance to get to know some of them a little better. We started our lessons, and our first was Navigation, with Miss Bonny.

She had a nasty face, just like the others, but she seemed nice enough. She made Molly and me sit at the front of the class, and kept asking us if we understood everything. We did, of course. The First Mate has always been brilliant at teaching us how to read charts and plot a course. In fact, what Miss Bonny was teaching the other children was so easy, we'd done it years ago.

'I can see ye are very good at this, Jim,'

she said after a while. 'Perhaps ye'd like to help me . . .'

Miss Bonny got me to stand by the blackboard. She pinned a large chart of the Caribbean on it, and told me to show the class how we planned our voyages on The Saucy Sally.

'Why don't ye just show us where ye've been recently,' she said, 'what islands ye've visited . . .'

I did what she asked. Miss Bonny seemed very interested in the chart once I'd finished.

Something similar happened in our next lesson, Gunnery, with Mr Thunder. Molly and I didn't really need to learn how to load and fire a ship's guns. We'd done it thousands of times before. But Mr Thunder, who was friendly now, seemed more interested in how many guns The Saucy Sally had than in teaching us anyway.

We had Arithmetic next, with Miss Read. That was easy, too. The lesson was about pirate money, and how you could tell what silver plate or jewels were worth. Miss Read said the best way of learning things like that was to write down what sort of treasure our parents had, and add it all up.

After that, it was time for lunch. We left

the classroom and walked down the main companionway to the mess-hall. Molly said we had to line up outside until the bell rang.

When we got there, Jasper was waiting at the door. I was going to try to talk to some of the other children before we went in to eat. But as soon as I saw Jasper, I knew it would be impossible. He stood at the head of the line staring down at Molly and me.

So you can imagine how I felt when the person behind me slipped a note into my hand. I didn't dare turn round or look at it. Then the bell rang and Jasper went into the mess-hall. I opened the piece of paper and glanced down quickly.

There was only one word on it.

'*Beware!*'

Chapter Three

In which Jim makes a discovery

'What do you think it means, then?' said Molly when we were alone. The whole school was supposed to be having a rest after lunch, and we had all been sent back to our own cabins. She was holding the note in her hand.

'I don't know,' I said. 'Pat Flint gave it to me, but I didn't get a chance to talk to her.'

'You can't talk to anyone in this place,' said Molly. 'I've never seen so many quiet children. There's something very fishy going on here.'

I'd been thinking exactly the same thing myself. I didn't know much about schools, but this one didn't feel right. Why did the teachers seem more interested in getting facts *out* of our heads than putting things *into* them?

'There's only one way we're going to find out anything,' said Molly. 'I'm going to have a look round. Maybe I can talk to Pat or some of the other kids.'

'I'll come with you,' I said. I didn't like the idea of us splitting up.

'Oh no you won't,' she said. 'It might be dangerous, so I'd better go on my own. I *am* the oldest, after all.'

'But . . .'

'I'll have none of your "buts", Jim Bluebeard,' she said. 'I'm going on my own, and that's an end of it.'

Molly can be very bossy sometimes. In fact, just like the Cap'n, there's no arguing with her once she's made her mind up.

She opened the door a crack. She looked up and down to make sure the coast was clear.

'I won't be long,' she whispered. She slipped out, softly shutting the door behind her.

I was alone, with nothing to do but wait for Molly to come back. I walked up and down the cabin, chewing my fingernails. I was getting more and more nervous. That word '*Beware*!' kept going round and round in my mind.

It was no good. I would have to go after her.

I opened the door and looked up and down, just as Molly had done. There was no one in sight, so I went out.

I hadn't gone far when I realised I had two problems. The first was that I didn't know where Molly had gone. And the second was that I didn't know my way round the school very well. But I wasn't going back now.

I was terrified I was going to meet one of the teachers, but I didn't. The companionways were silent.

Then I heard a noise that nearly made me leap out of my skin. It sounded like somebody laughing, a nasty, cruel, vicious laugh. It was coming from a room a little further down. There was a sign on the door that said 'Captain's Cabin'.

I crept past, and saw some stairs. I

21

thought they might lead me to Molly, so I went up them. At the top was another door. I opened it carefully, and found myself on the roof of the school. It looked like the upper deck of a ship, with gunwales round the edges, masts and rigging.

In front of me were a couple of hatches. I went over to one, and discovered it was filled in with glass. I could see through it to the Captain's cabin below. I looked down . . . and saw all the teachers — Miss Prudence, Jasper, and the rest!

They were sitting round a chart table smoking big pipes and swigging grog. And from the way they were laughing, they must have thought something was very funny.

I was lucky. They hadn't spotted me. So, holding my breath, I lifted the hatch a crack to hear what they were saying.

''Tis a devilish fine plan, Katie,' said Mr Thunder to the person I'd known till now as Miss Prudence. 'And only a pirate as crafty and cunning as ye could think of it.'

'Ye be right there, messmate,' said Miss Bonny. 'Only Cut-Throat Katie could think of opening a school for pirate kiddies. Their stupid mums and dads bring their precious babies here, all unsuspecting . . .'

'And we scare the poor little things so much they daren't even talk to each other,' said Miss Read. 'Then we make them tell us where the family treasure's buried!' They all started laughing again.

So that was what they were up to! Everything fell into place now, and I remembered what I'd heard about Cut-Throat Katie and her crew. They were the scum of the seven seas, villains who tricked and cheated everyone they came across.

'And now we've got those Bluebeards my plan is nearly complete,' said Katie with a cackle. 'We won't start giving them the frightening treatment for another day or two. Let them settle in first . . . Then as soon as we find out what we want to know, we can ransom them and all the others.'

'But ye said I could rip some arms and legs off,' mumbled Jasper in a deep, rumbling voice. He sounded very disappointed.

'Ah, they don't call 'ee The Giant Jasper Blood for nothing, do they?' said Cut-Throat Katie. 'Don't worry, Jasper, I'll let 'ee have one or two of the smaller ones to play with. I don't think we'll get much for that Jim Bluebeard, for instance . . .'

That was enough for me. I turned to run away, but in my fear I must have slipped. I tried to stay on my feet, but I couldn't.

I fell right through the hatch.

With a great crash and a tinkling of smashed glass, I landed on the chart table in the cabin below!

Chapter Four

In which Jim walks the plank

The cabin was in an uproar. The chart table had collapsed beneath me, and all the bottles of grog had been smashed. Several of Cut-Throat Katie's crew had fallen over backwards in their chairs, and everyone was shouting.

'Avast there!' screamed Katie from the deck. She'd been knocked flat and was pinned down by the top of the table. 'Action stations! All hands grab that lad!'

Jasper tried to catch me, but I was too

27

quick for him. I rolled on to the floor and squirmed right through Mr Thunder's legs.

But I was just a second too late. Miss Bonny slammed the door, and stood facing me with her back to it. I turned round, and found myself staring down the barrels of two pistols held by Miss Read. I slowly raised my hands.

'Nice of ye to drop in on us, Master Bluebeard,' said Cut-Throat Katie with a ghastly smile. Jasper pushed the wreckage to one side and helped her up. 'Jasper, tie up our little guest. Thunder, go and fetch that big sister of his . . . We'd better find out what both of them know.'

'Aye aye, Katie,' said Thunder. He opened the door and scuttled out. Jasper tied my hands very tightly behind my back, but I didn't care. They might have caught me, but they obviously didn't know where

28

Molly was, and that made me glad. I just hoped she could escape. Then at least one of us might get back safely to the Cap'n and the First Mate.

Cut-Throat Katie was *furious* when Thunder told her Molly wasn't in our cabin.

'I thought I told 'ee to keep a weather eye on their cabin!' she screamed. 'Having this little rascal snooping where he's not wanted is bad enough, but now you tell me his sister's gone missing too! Well, Thunder, ye'd better find her, or I'll have your guts for garters!'

'Aye aye, Katie,' said Thunder with a gulp. He looked very pale. The eye that wasn't covered by a patch started twitching. 'I'll find her!' He shot out of the door again, and Katie turned to me.

'Now then, Master Bluebeard,' she said. She wasn't screaming any more, but her voice was even more scary now it was quiet. 'What are you and your sister up to? I should have known ye Bluebeards would be trouble.'

'I won't tell you anything,' I said. 'I don't care what you do, you won't get a word out of me.'

Katie just laughed. It was that nasty, cruel, vicious laugh I'd heard from the companionway.

'Oh, I think ye'll talk all right,' she said, 'once ye see what we've got lined up. It's time he had his first swimming lesson, isn't it, messmates?'

The others all started giggling.

'I don't need any lessons,' I said. 'I can swim already.'

'Is that so?' said Katie with a cackle. 'Well this is a *special* swimming lesson. The sort of lesson ye'll only need to do once. Lead the way, Jasper.'

We left the Captain's Cabin and walked down the companionway. Soon we were in a part of the school I didn't recognise. It was a bit darker than elsewhere, and I thought about making a run for it. But I realised I wouldn't get very far, not with my hands tied and Miss Read pointing those pistols at me.

At last we came to a door. Jasper unlocked it, and we went out into bright sunshine.

I was dazzled to begin with, but my eyes cleared after a while. I was standing on the edge of a pirate swimming pool, and even though I was scared, I could see it was amazing. There were a couple of big slides, some diving boards, a small island with palm trees in the middle, and lots of sun beds round the sides.

'Not bad, eh?' said Cut-Throat Katie. 'This is our staff room. It's where the crew and me come to relax after a hard day with you blasted kids. But sometimes we let our little pets have a swim instead. Show him, Jasper.'

Jasper knelt down and pulled up what looked like a gate in the edge of the pool. A lot of small, dark shapes swam out into the sparkling water. I didn't like the look of

them at all. I noticed even Jasper pulled his hand out of their way quickly.

'There they go . . .' said Katie. 'A nice little shoal of piranhas, the nastiest, hungriest fish in the world. I think we'll give them an appetiser first . . .'

Katie opened a small cupboard and took out a large piece of meat. It had a string attached to it. She lowered the meat into the water, which seemed to boil for a second or two. When she pulled the string up, all that was left on the end was a shining white bone. Cut-Throat Katie waved the bone in my face.

'Now, are you ready to talk, Master Bluebeard?' she said.

I gulped, but I said nothing.

'Right, you little whelp,' she said, 'on to the plank with ye!'

Jasper drew a big cutlass and prodded me towards one of the diving boards. He kept prodding me until I was standing at the end. It felt very wobbly and unsafe. My knees started to knock together. I tried not to look down into the water below.

'Is your tongue feeling any looser *now*?' called out Katie.

I still didn't say anything. Besides, my tongue wasn't feeling loose. It was bone dry with fear.

'Very well,' she screamed. 'Jasper, you know what to do . . .'

Chapter Five

In which there's a mutiny!

I stood on the end of the diving board with my eyes closed. Any second now, I thought, Jasper would prod me again. The last thing I'd hear would be the splash as I plunged into the pool. And that would be the end of Jim Bluebeard.

But there was no splash. Instead, I heard someone shouting.

'Lay down your cutlass, Jasper! We've got you covered!'

It was Molly! I'd never been so glad to hear her voice.

I opened my eyes. Coming round the other end of the pool was a crowd of pirate children, with Molly leading them. Behind her were Polly and Pat Flint, the Teach brothers, and lots more. It looked like the whole school was there. They were all armed, some with cutlasses, others with muskets or pistols.

And Molly was pointing her pistol straight at Jasper.

'This be mutiny!' screeched Katie. 'Get back to your cabins!'

'It certainly is!' said Molly. 'Now let my brother go!'

'She means it, Katie,' Mr Thunder called out. I hadn't noticed him at first, but there he was, standing tied up between the Teach brothers. 'They're going to break out!'

'Oh, are they?' said Katie. 'Over my dead body!'

'That can be arranged!' shouted Molly. I could see she was losing her temper. 'Let's get 'em, everybody! Charge!'

The children swarmed towards Katie and her crew. Behind me I could hear Jasper growling. I turned round, and saw his attention was on Molly and the others. Now was my chance.

I put my head down and ran towards him as fast as I could. He had lowered the cutlass, so there was no chance of me getting stuck on the end of it. He never saw me coming. My head hit him in the stomach, and he flew backwards through the air. He landed with a crash by the side of the swimming pool. I came down on top of him, rolled over and got to my feet.

By then Molly and the others had started fighting with Katie and her crew. It was all confusion. Cutlasses whistled and clanged, pistols and muskets went off with loud

bangs, and everyone was shouting and cursing. With my hands tied, all I could do was try and keep out of the way.

'It's no good, Katie,' Miss Bonny shouted after a while. 'There's too many of them!'

'Retreat, then!' screamed Katie. 'Retreat!'

Step by step, Cut-Throat Katie and the others fought their way back to the door. Jasper was with them now, and somehow they'd managed to get hold of Mr Thunder again. It was touch and go, but they got out in the end. Jasper slammed the door. We heard it being locked and bolted from inside.

'Break it down!' shouted Tom Teach. 'They've kept us scared too long. Now it's our turn to frighten *them*!'

Everybody cheered and started hammering and banging on the door. Molly meanwhile was getting me untied and making sure I was all right. Then she shouted above the noise.

'I've got a better idea,' she said. 'Let's get away and tell our parents what Katie and her crew have been doing. They'll come back and really teach *them* a thing or two about being pirates!'

Pat Flint said she knew just the thing to get us off the island. She'd heard Mr Thunder and Miss Read talking the other day about the academy's jolly-boat. It was kept in the harbour, and was supposed to be used for school outings. But of course it never was.

Now as you know, although a jolly-boat's a small craft with a mast and sails, it can take quite a few people. So it sounded perfect for us. We set off immediately.

On our way to the harbour, Molly explained what she'd done after she'd left our cabin. She'd found Polly and Pat, and they had told her that Cut-Throat Katie was definitely up to something wicked. They'd decided then and there to start a mutiny.

They'd rounded up all the other children, and raided the armoury for weapons. They'd caught Mr Thunder while he was looking for Molly, and found out from him what Katie probably had in mind for me. That's why they'd headed straight for the pool.

41

Then I told her everything I knew, and how I'd ended up walking the plank. Although she was cross that I'd disobeyed her, we didn't have time to argue.

Pretty soon I was counting everyone safely aboard the jolly-boat. There were 20 of us altogether. It was a tight squeeze, but Molly said she thought we could make it. Then she started giving out orders.

'Take the wheel, Jim,' she said. 'You're good at steering. You others, weigh anchor, and run up some sail. Let's get out of here!'

The jolly-boat proved to be quite speedy. It wasn't long before we started dipping into the big waves beyond the harbour entrance. Soon we would be in the open sea.

'Free at last!' shouted Polly Flint. 'We've escaped!'

But she was wrong.

'Vessel on the starboard bow!' called out Tim Teach from the crow's nest. We all looked in the direction he was pointing.

A large pirate ship was coming round the headland. Fluttering from its tallest mast was a black flag bearing the face of a grinning shark.

'It's The Shark's Revenge,' said Tom Teach. 'That's Cut-Throat Katie's ship! They must have had it hidden on the other side of the island!'

And it was bearing down on us, getting closer all the time . . .

Chapter Six

In which a sea-battle takes place

The Shark's Revenge was the biggest pirate ship I'd ever seen. It was bristling with guns, and they were all pointing in one direction — *ours*.

'Ahoy there, ye rascals!' It was Cut-Throat Katie. I could see her standing on the poop-deck, surrounded by her scurvy crew. 'Hove to or we'll blow you out of the water!'

'You couldn't blow up a balloon, you old rat-bag!' I shouted back. Everyone on the jolly-boat laughed, but Katie didn't think it was very funny.

'Just you wait till I've got my hands on 'ee, Jim Bluebeard,' she spluttered. 'I'll teach you to make fun of me.'

'You'll have to catch us first,' shouted Molly.

We didn't stop to talk any more. We knew our only hope was to out-run them, and the sooner we put up more sail the better.

Everyone worked together, and soon we were flying over the waves. From time to time there were puffs of smoke on The Shark's Revenge and cannon balls whistled towards us. They all splashed harmlessly into the sea.

But they were still gaining on us. With 20 of us in the boat, we'd never get away. We thought making it lighter might help. So we threw everything overboard that we could,

and for a while the gap between us and The
Shark's Revenge got wider.

Then it started to narrow again. We
could hear Katie cackling and shouting
curses at us. We could see her crew
capering on the decks, waving their
cutlasses and firing their pistols into the air.
And each cannon ball they fired landed
closer.

'It's no good,' said Molly at last. 'We'll never get away!'

'Hang on, Molly,' I said. I'd seen something over her shoulder, on the far horizon.

'We'll never let them take us alive, though, will we?' she said.

'Molly, I think . . .' The dot on the horizon was getting bigger.

'This looks like the end, Jim,' said Molly as a cannon ball landed too close for comfort. Spray from the splash drenched us. 'I'm sorry I've been horrible to you sometimes. I didn't really mean . . .'

'Molly, will you please shut up and just *look*!' I shouted in the end. I swung her round and pointed at the dot, which had now become another pirate ship. 'It's The Saucy Sally!'

'I don't believe you,' said Molly, peering into the distance. Then she started to smile. 'It can't be . . . it is! We're safe!'

'Not yet, we're not!' I said.

The Shark's Revenge was just behind us. But they'd seen The Saucy Sally coming towards their port bow. Katie and her crew started moving round their guns, but they were too late. There was a puff of smoke from The Saucy Sally, a cannon ball whistled through the air . . . and brought a mast right down on top of them!

'Three cheers for the Cap'n and the First Mate!' I shouted. 'Hip, hip, hurray!'

A moment later we were pulling up alongside The Saucy Sally. The First Mate threw down a rope ladder and, one by one, we all climbed aboard. Molly and I hugged and kissed our parents. Then we poured out our story.

'But how did you know we were in danger?' I said at last. I couldn't understand why they'd come back so soon.

'Er . . . we didn't know, Jim lad,' said the Cap'n. He looked a little embarrassed. 'The truth is, we did miss the pair of ye. It just wasn't the same without 'ee . . .'

'The Cap'n is right,' said the First Mate. 'We decided we'd rather have you with us, even if you do argue all the time.'

Molly and I smiled at each other, and then we hugged the Cap'n and the First Mate again. We were so glad to be home.

'This be very nice, me hearties,' said the Cap'n at last, 'but let's save the hugging for later. We've a job to do.'

He pointed towards The Shark's Revenge. They must have recovered, for they looked as if they were getting ready to give us a broadside.

'All hands to the guns!' called out the First Mate. Molly and I led the other children to the gun deck. We soon got the guns loaded.

'Ready . . .' called out the Cap'n. 'Aim . . . FIRE!'

We let off a huge broadside. When the smoke cleared, we saw something that started us cheering again.

The Shark's Revenge was sinking!

We sailed away, leaving Cut-Throat Katie and her crew crammed into their dinghy. They shouted and shook their fists at us, but we just laughed.

'Well, they've learned their lesson,' said the Cap'n. 'And so have we, I'll be bound. In future, us Bluebeards had better stick together. Now, what say we have a pirate party before we take your friends back to their mums and dads? Those in favour, say aye!'

'AYE!' we all shouted, as loud as we could.

'I'll choose the games!' I said.

'No you won't, I will . . .' said Molly.

'Ah, do ye hear that, First Mate?' said the Cap'n with a smile. The First Mate was smiling too. 'The scallywags be arguing already. 'Tis music to me ears . . .'

We all laughed — and then we had the best pirate party there's ever been!

ADVENTURE ON SKULL ISLAND

Tony Bradman

Life for a pirate family is one long adventure!

When Jim finds a treasure map of Skull Island on board the *Saucy Sally*, he knows he and his sister Molly are in for an exciting time. But little do they know that their great enemy, Captain Swagg, is after the same treasure – and is determined to get there first!

Also in Young Puffin

ONE NIL

Tony Bradman

Dave Brown is football mad!

All Dave ever thinks about is football,
even in the classroom. He just can't
concentrate on anything else! So imagine
Dave's excitement when he finds out the
England squad are coming to train at his
local club! He desperately wants to go
and see them – but what about school?
At first it seems impossible, but then
Dave works out an ingenious plan – a
plan that leads him to scoring the goal of
a lifetime!

Also in Young Puffin

Admiral Fatso FitzPugwash

John Ryan

"Fatso the Fathead! He's useless! Greedy, stupid, cowardly . . . !"

The Baron Fatsophilus FitzPugwash (Fatso for short) is a recently discovered ancestor of Captain Pugwash, and fans of that notorious pirate will instantly spot the family likeness.

Poor Fatso. First he's made Admiral of the Fleet – and he's *terrified* of water; then he's ordered to feed and entertain the King and his court of a thousand – but he *hates* spending any money.

Young readers will love the hilarious pictures and text in this very entertaining pair of adventures.

The Go-Ahead GANG

Robert Swindells

The gang members were Don, Kath, Mick, Renee, Georgy – and me. I'm Bob, and I want to tell you about some of the stuff we did.

The Go-Ahead Gang spent a lot of time looking for things to do, and some of the things they did led them into danger, or into trouble.

There was the time they explored a mysterious dark tunnel; and the time they had the fastest sledge ride ever; and the time Bob and Don played on an RAF firing range.

These are exciting and fun stories by an award-winning story-teller.

Ricky's Summertime Christmas Present

Frank Rodgers

FOR RICKY BROWN. DO NOT WAIT UNTIL CHRISTMAS. OPEN NOW!

Ricky is puzzled to receive a Christmas present in the middle of summer from an uncle he didn't know he had. But the present leads him on an exciting adventure to rescue his long-lost uncle from danger.

READ MORE IN PUFFIN

For children of all ages, Puffin represents quality and variety – the very best in publishing today around the world.

For complete information about books available from Puffin – and Penguin – and how to order them, contact us at the appropriate address below. Please note that for copyright reasons the selection of books varies from country to country.

On the world wide web: www.penguin.co.uk

In the United Kingdom: Please write to *Dept. EP, Penguin Books Ltd, Bath Road, Harmondsworth, West Drayton, Middlesex UB7 ODA*
Schools Line in the UK: Please write to

In the United States: Please write to *Consumer Sales, Penguin USA, P.O. Box 999, Dept. 17109, Bergenfield, New Jersey 07621-0120.* VISA and MasterCard holders call 1-800-253-6476 to order Penguin titles

In Canada: Please write to *Penguin Books Canada Ltd, 10 Alcorn Avenue, Suite 300, Toronto, Ontario M4V 3B2*

In Australia: Please write to *Penguin Books Australia Ltd, P.O. Box 257, Ringwood, Victoria 3134*

In New Zealand: Please write to *Penguin Books (NZ) Ltd, Private Bag 102902, North Shore Mail Centre, Auckland 10*

In India: Please write to *Penguin Books India Pvt Ltd, 706 Eros Apartments, 56 Nehru Place, New Delhi 110 019*

In the Netherlands: Please write to *Penguin Books Netherlands bv, Postbus 3507, NL-1001 AH Amsterdam*

In Germany: Please write to *Penguin Books Deutschland GmbH, Metzlerstrasse 26, 60594 Frankfurt am Main*

In Spain: Please write to *Penguin Books S. A., Bravo Murillo 19, 1° B, 28015 Madrid*

In Italy: Please write to *Penguin Italia s.r.l., Via Felice Casati 20, I–20124 Milano*

In France: Please write to *Penguin France S. A., 17 rue Lejeune, F–31000 Toulouse*

In Japan: Please write to *Penguin Books Japan, Ishikiribashi Building, 2–5–4, Suido, Bunkyo-ku, Tokyo 112*

In South Africa: Please write to *Longman Penguin Southern Africa (Pty) Ltd, Private Bag X08, Bertsham 2013*